The Girl Who Changed Her Fate

A retelling
of a Greek
folktale

Atheneum 1992 New York

Maxwell Macmillan Canada
Toronto

Maxwell Macmillan International
New York Oxford Singapore Sydney

The Girl Who Changed Her Fate

Laura Marshall

For Antonio
—L. M.

Atheneum
Macmillan Publishing Company
866 Third Avenue
New York, NY 10022

Maxwell Macmillan Canada, Inc.
1200 Eglinton Avenue East
Suite 200
Don Mills, Ontario M3C 3N1

Macmillan Publishing Company is part of the Maxwell Communication
Group of Companies.

First edition

Printed in Hong Kong
10 9 8 7 6 5 4 3 2 1
The text of this book is set in 14 point Janson.
The illustrations are rendered in oil paint.

LIBRARY OF CONGRESS CATALOGING-IN-PUBLICATION DATA

Marshall, Laura.
    The girl who changed her fate/by Laura Marshall.—1st ed.
        p.   cm.
        Summary: Ill-fated Eleni travels to the house where all the fates
live and battles to change her lot in life.
        ISBN 0-689-31742-5
        [1. Folklore—Greece.]   I. Title.
PZ8.1.M3557Gi   1992
398.2—dc20
    [E]   91–23137

There was once a widow who had three
daughters. The girls were kind, intelligent,
and beautiful. Each of them wanted to be
married, yet they were never courted by
any of the young men in their town.

One morning in autumn an old woman came limping down the road toward the widow's house. She rang the bell and begged for some pennies. Seeing her shivering in the doorway, the widow said, "You must be cold! Come in and warm yourself."

As they sat at the kitchen table, drinking tea and eating apples, the widow talked about her daughters.

"I'm so worried about them," she said. "They are good girls, but I don't understand why none of the young men come to see them."

The old woman listened, nodding her head. Then she said, "Tonight, when the girls are sleeping, go in and look at them. Especially look at each one's hands. I'll return here tomorrow and then you can tell me what you saw."

Late that night the widow got up from
her bed and tiptoed down the hall to look
at her daughters as they slept. The oldest
girl had her hands under her head. The sec-
ond daughter had her hands folded on her
heart. The youngest was sleeping with her
hands on her lap.

The following day the old woman returned, and the widow told her what she had seen.

"Ah, it's your youngest who is troubled! She is ill-fated!" the old woman said. "Each of us has a fate. When a person is born, that fate makes a promise to help and guide one. A good-hearted fate means a happy life! But sometimes a fate forgets her promise and becomes wild and cruel. Then the life of the person will be bitter. Your youngest daughter's fate is blocking the happiness of the other two. If anything is to change, the youngest must leave this house." The old woman shook her head sadly and went on her way.

When she was gone, the youngest girl, whose name was Eleni, came to her mother.

"I heard everything," she said. "I have decided that I must leave. Please, won't you help me to get ready?"

The widow protested, but Eleni persuaded her that it was the best thing to do. They sewed her dowry of gold coins into the hem of her skirt. Then Eleni dressed herself as a wandering nun and was ready to leave.

Even as she kissed her family good-bye, suitors were approaching the house, bringing gifts for her sisters.

As Eleni traveled, each day carried the cold breath of winter's approach. She went from town to town, living on the charity of people who cared to show her kindness. Among those was a cloth merchant, who one evening gave her a meal and let her sleep in his shop.

In the darkest hour of that night Eleni's
fate came to torment her. The fate ripped
bolts of fabric down from the shelves. She
tore and shredded the cloth, and destroyed
everything she touched. Terrified, Eleni
pleaded with her to stop, but the fate only
screamed, "Be quiet or I'll tear you limb
from limb!"

In the morning the merchant came down and saw his destroyed shop. Bewildered, he could only say, "What have you done? You have ruined me!"

There was little that Eleni could say. She took a coin from her hem and gave it to the merchant. Then she went on her way, leaving him shaking his head.

In another town a glass merchant took her in. Once again her fate found her and shattered everything in the shop. Amid the crashing and splintering glass Eleni begged her to stop. "Quiet!! or I'll break every bone in your body!" the fate roared.

In the morning Eleni gave the distraught glass merchant a coin from her hem and left the town in shame.

Eleni wandered on. As snow began to whiten the mountains she came to a queen's house, where she asked if she could work until spring. The queen saw at once that Eleni was not a wandering nun at all, but a distressed and tormented girl, far from home.

"Can you embroider with pearls?" she asked.

When Eleni said that she could, she was taken into the house and given a place to sit near the fire.

But whenever Eleni began to work, her basket of threads and pearls was over-turned. Wherever she was sitting, figures from the paintings leaped from the frames and pulled her hair. Often strange sounds were heard in empty rooms, for Eleni's fate had found her and still tormented her.

In the months that followed, the servants often complained to the queen.

"Ever since that girl has been in this house everything has gone wrong! The pots fall from where they're hung and plates slide off the shelves!" said one.

"The chickens leave no eggs, the cow will give no milk, and the cat will catch no mice!"

"What are we to do?!" they all cried together.

The queen always said to them, "We must be kind to this girl and have patience with her, for she is ill-fated."

One day when Eleni and the queen were alone, the queen said, "You cannot go on like this. You must do something to change your fate."

She took Eleni to the window and pointed to a mountain in the distance.

"You see that mountain, Eleni? That is where all of the fates of the world live together. You must go there and seek out your fate. When you find her, offer her a gift and ask her to change your fate. But be sure not to leave until she has taken the gift from you and kept it!"

The queen gave Eleni some bread to offer her fate, and before long she was walking up the misty, rugged path that wound around the mountain.

At last she came to a house surrounded by a walled garden.

"This must be the house of the fates," thought Eleni, so she went to the door and knocked.

It was opened by a woman with clear, quiet eyes.

"I am looking for my fate," said Eleni, "but you are not mine."

The woman nodded and closed the door. Eleni knocked at the door many more times, and with every knock a different fate answered. But not one of them was hers.

Then she knocked once more. Scarcely
had she touched the door when it flew
open and a wild-eyed woman strode from
it, glaring at Eleni.

"Why did you come here?!" she
shrieked.

Frightened as she was, Eleni held the
bread out and cried: "Fate, who has made
my fate, change my fate!"

The fate grabbed the bread from her and
threw it on the ground. "No! I shall not
change it! To change your fate you must die
and be born again!"

Eleni picked up the bread, held it out to
her fate again, and repeated her plea. But
the fate cursed and threw handfuls of dirt
in Eleni's face.

When some of the other fates came to see what the trouble was, their hearts were moved with pity.

"Oh, come now," they said to Eleni's fate, "show some mercy! Why must you torment her so? Remember your promise to help her."

Their efforts were useless. Eleni continued to offer the bread to her fate, who hurled insults back at her and refused to accept it.

But then, exhausted by her raging, the fate stopped. In that moment of quiet, she saw Eleni's innocence and persistence, and her heart softened. When Eleni held out the bread again, her fate took it—and kept it!

She then took a ball of silk thread from her pocket.

"Take this thread and keep it!" she said. "But if someone should come seeking it, you must demand its weight in gold—or better!" She threw the thread at Eleni, who caught it and ran.

Eleni returned to the queen's house, and as winter turned to spring she found that all the torments of her fate had ceased.

In the village near the queen's house, there was a family preparing for their daughter's wedding. But the seamstresses had run out of silk thread before the bride's dress was finished. They had heard that a girl at the queen's house had a ball of silk thread, so the bride's brother offered to go and buy it.

"How much will you take for your thread?" the young man asked Eleni.

"I'll only exchange it for its weight in gold—or better!" she answered.

"Fair enough," said the young man. They put the thread on one side of a scale and then put pieces of gold on the other side. But even when all the gold had been put on, the side with the thread had not moved at all. Then the young man's eyes lit up and he stepped onto the scale himself. There was a perfect balance!

"Well," he said, "if we are to have the thread, then you must have me!"

Eleni laughed and agreed.

Later that summer Eleni and the young
man were married. Their wedding was
fine, with lots of singing and dancing. After
that they lived a long life together, rich in
generosity and friendships.

And may we live just as well!